JAMIE LEE CURTIS & LAURA CORNELL

My
Brave Year
of
Firsts

Tries, Sighs,
and
High Fives

Joanna Cotler Books
An Imprint of HarperCollins Publishers

The **first** time I rode a two-wheeler alone,
I crashed and my mom filmed it on her iPhone.
I crashed and I crashed. Dad ran out of steam.
He let go, I went straight.
Mom filmed as she screamed.

I got my first pet, a rescued Lab, Keith.
I chose him 'cause we were both missing front teeth.

"I'll take care of him," I said with a boast.
Till the first time I picked up his poop—it was GROSS!

The first day I walked straight into first grade.
My teacher, Miss Apple, said, "Don't be afraid."
At first I felt like I might not fit in,

then I made my first friends, my very FIRST twins.

I struggled at *first* to learn to tie shoes.
My sweet Auntie Cookie showed me choices to use:
Bunny Ears, Classic, Loop-over-under-through.

Bunny Ears

Classic

Loop-over-under-through

Loop through
many times
beneath
and up
and
REPEAT

Zip
and
pretend

Tape it

Clip-on

Twist and
criss-cross

Fancy

I tried and tried till at last I could, too.

I took riding lessons
on a pony called Ace.
The first time I fell,
I got a scrape on my face.
But then I held on and I learned how to trot,
that "giddyup" is to go
and "whoa" is to stop.

First grade was fun,
  new firsts every day,
    what a homonym was,
      what elephants weigh.

weigh

(that a)
way

hair

hare

piece

peace

stole  stole

Not all firsts were fun. Some firsts were hard.
When I stole Zoë's pencil,
I couldn't play in the yard.

fair  fare

(un) fair

WHAT I
STOLE TODAY

I asked for permission from my parents to walk
with Keith and the twins, first time 'round my block.

We took some supplies and carried Mom's phone.
We felt all grown up to be out on our own.

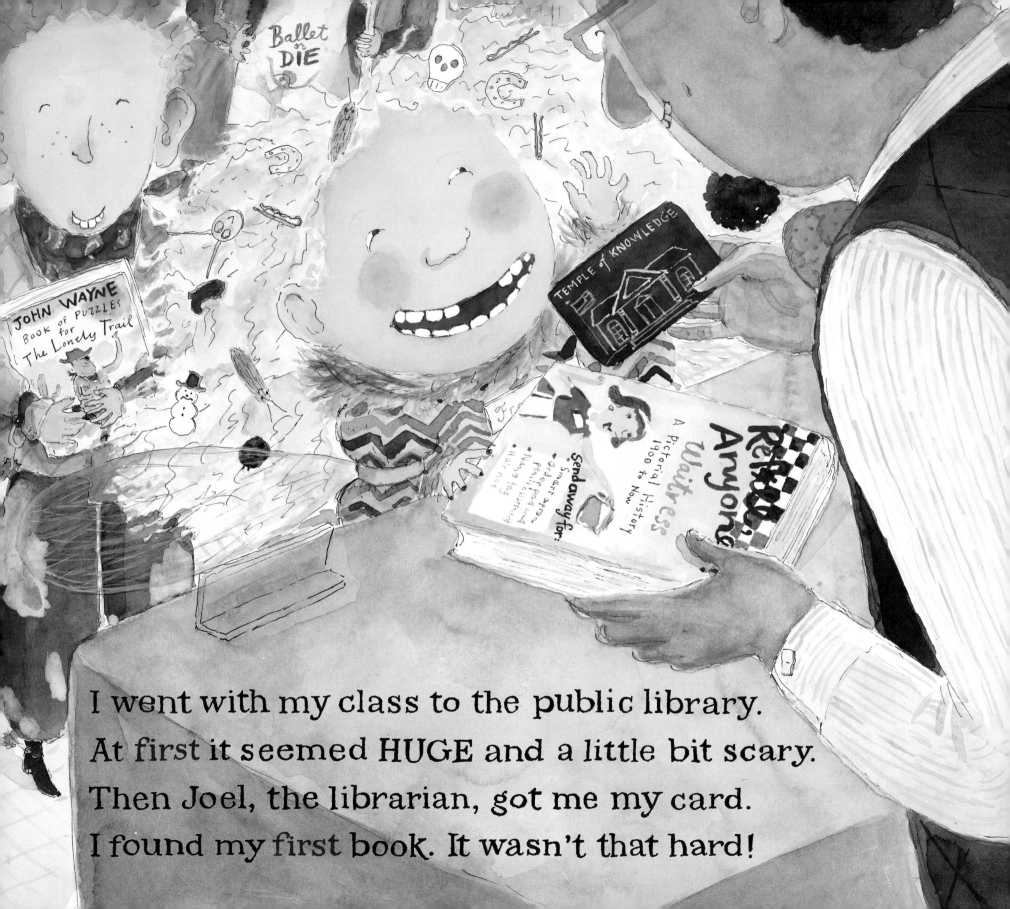

I went with my class to the public library.
At first it seemed HUGE and a little bit scary.
Then Joel, the librarian, got me my card.
I found my first book. It wasn't that hard!

I also got caught in my very first lie.
My parents were cross. I started to cry.
I learned a first lesson, that to stand up and say
I did something wrong starts to make it OK.

For the very first time
    I worked with my father.
At his restaurant I would not be a bother.
I put out the HOT sauce
    that makes your ears steam.
As a waitress I was a real part of his team.

My firsts kept on coming—

my first
pony show,

my first tummy flu that made me go
and go . . .
       and go . . .

my first big girl heels
that made me feel tall,

my first ballet class,

my first game of T-ball.

ATHLON

A fabulous first? My TRY-Athlon medal!
For my age and group, a swim, run, and pedal.
I raced against time. It was quite a test.
While some tried to win, I just tried my best.

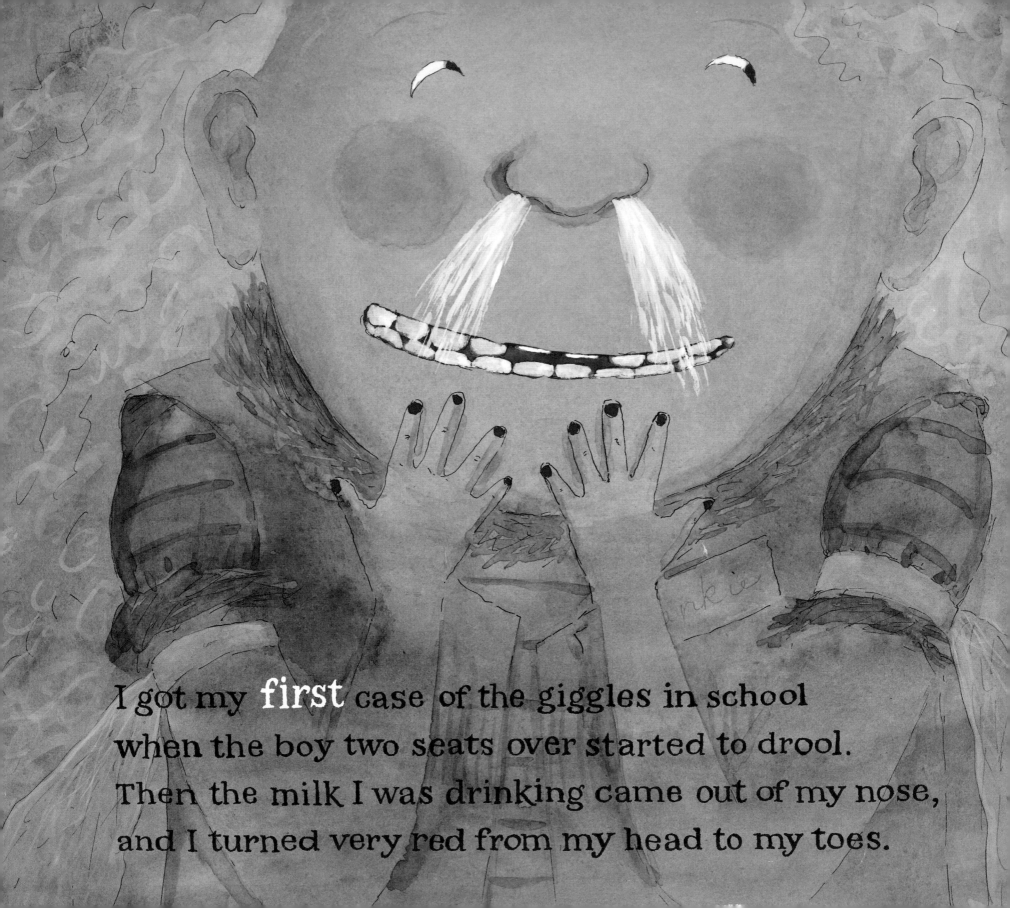

I got my **first** case of the giggles in school
when the boy two seats over started to drool.
Then the milk I was drinking came out of my nose,
and I turned very red from my head to my toes.

I wanted to learn to make a rope skip,
but for all of my tries I just learned to trip.
It was very hard to connect hands and feet—
till the first time it worked.
It was quite a feat!

I found a small beetle who was missing a leg.
I got him a box and I named him Greg.
I punched a few holes to save him from cats.
I added some grass—

my first

bug habitat.

I got my *first* bee sting, and boy, did it hurt.
I shouldn't have walked barefoot in the dirt.

I sold some flat rocks that I painted and signed.
And I made a donation for the very first time.

I tried for the first time to taste my mom's truffles
that apparently come from when pigs use their snuffles.
She put them in pasta with broccoli stems.
"Try it," she said, but I'll NEVER like them.

At the end of the summer I tubed on my own.
I bounced on the water like a skipping stone.
The lake was all glassy—smooth, dark, and cold.
I held on and signaled just like I was told.

And after the s'mores we camped by the lake.
My very first tent that my dad let *me* stake.
All cozy and warm in my bag with a pad,

I thought about all
the fun firsts
I'd had.

And I climbed the BIG rock. I was old enough now.
My dad showed me step-by-step so I'd know how.
I looked down at the lake. I jumped out without fear.
When I came up and smiled, the entire lake cheered!

Some firsts just happen.
Some come when I try.
Some firsts make me smile.
Some firsts make me cry.

But I knew at that moment—
though I've known all along—
that
first things
first happen
when I'm
brave,
true,
and strong.

To Frankie and Zoë, both brave and bold.
—J.L.C.

To my adventurous parents, who gave me the firsts,
supported my mishaps, and celebrated my successes.
—L.C.

High fives to Heidi, Carla, Phyllis, Alyson, Lucille, Dorothy, Kathryn, and the HC and
JLC teams, and a top ten to Laura and Joanna for our 10th book together. —J.L.C.

To all at HC who create big magic in small spaces, and to Phyllis for taking care of me.
And a thank-you never big enough to Jamie and Joanna. —L.C.

Books to Grow By is a trademark of Jamie Lee Curtis.
My Brave Year of Firsts: Tries, Sighs, and High Fives
Text copyright © 2012 by Jamie Lee Curtis
Illustrations copyright © 2012 by Laura Cornell
All rights reserved. Printed in the United States of America.
No part of this book may be used or reproduced in any manner whatsoever without written permission except in the
case of brief quotations embodied in critical articles and reviews. For information address HarperCollins Children's Books,
a division of HarperCollins Publishers, 10 East 53rd Street, New York, NY 10022. www.harpercollinschildrens.com

Library of Congress Cataloging-in-Publication Data is available.
ISBN 978-0-06-144155-4 (trade bdg.)

12 13 14 15 16 LP 10 9 8 7 6 5 4 3 2 1 ❖ First Edition